TAR

CROWN PUBLISHERS, INC., NEW YORK·

BEACH

FAITH RINGGOLD

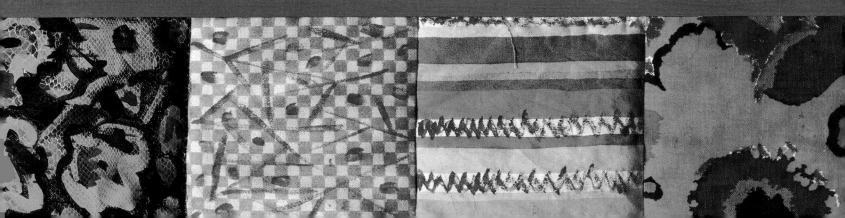

Published by Crown Publishers, Inc., a Random House company, 225
Park Avenue South, New York, New York 10003
CROWN is a trademark of Crown Publishers, Inc.
Manufactured in the United States of America

Library of Congress Cataloging-in-Publication Data
Ringgold, Faith. Tar beach / Faith Ringgold.
   p.   cm.
Summary: A young girl dreams of flying above her Harlem home,
claiming all she sees for herself and her family. Based on the author's
quilt painting of the same name.
[1. Harlem (New York, N.Y.)–Fiction. 2. Afro-Americans–Fiction.
3. Flight–Fiction. 4. Dreams–Fiction.] I. Title.
PZ7.R4726Tar 1991   [E]–dc20   90-40410

ISBN 0-517-58030-6 (trade)
    0-517-58031-4 (lib bdg.)

10 9 8 7 6 5 4

My first book is for my mother, Mme.
Willi Posey, who took me to Tar Beach. And
everywhere else. If she could be here now!

And for my three grandchildren, Faith,
Theodora, and Martha. They are all strong
readers and can fly.

And for my children, Michele and Barbara.
They are women now. But I knew them when.

And for my dealer and friend, Bernice
Steinbaum, who just keeps me up in the air.

And for my husband, Burdette Ringgold,
who keeps my feet on the ground. It was he
who reminded me about Tar Beach after all
these years.

I will always remember when the stars fell down around me
and lifted me up above the George Washington Bridge.

I could see our tiny rooftop, with Mommy and Daddy
and Mr. and Mrs. Honey, our next-door neighbors,
still playing cards as if nothing was going on,

and Be Be, my baby brother, lying real still on the mattress,
just like I told him to, his eyes like huge floodlights
tracking me through the sky.

Sleeping on Tar Beach was magical. Lying on the roof in
the night, with stars and skyscraper buildings all around me,
made me feel rich, like I owned all that I could see.

The bridge was my most prized possession.

Daddy said that the George Washington Bridge is the longest and most beautiful bridge in the world and that it opened in 1931, on the very day I was born.

Daddy worked on that bridge, hoisting cables. Since then,
I've wanted that bridge to be mine.

Now I have claimed it. All I had to do was fly over it for it to be mine forever. I can wear it like a giant diamond necklace,

or just fly above it and marvel at its sparkling beauty.
I can fly—yes, fly. Me, Cassie Louise Lightfoot, only eight
years old and in the third grade, and I can fly. That means
I am free to go wherever I want for the rest of my life.

Daddy took me to see the new union building he is
working on.

He can walk on steel girders high up in the sky and not fall. They call him the Cat.

But still he can't join the union because Grandpa wasn't a member.

Well, Daddy is going to own that building, 'cause I'm gonna fly over it and give it to him. Then it won't matter that he's not in their old union, or whether he's colored or a half-breed Indian, like they say.

He'll be rich and won't have to stand on 24-story-high girders and look down. He can look at his building going up.

And Mommy won't cry all winter when he goes to look for work and doesn't come home.

And Mommy can laugh and sleep late like Mrs. Honey,

and we can have ice cream every night for dessert.

E CREAM FACTORY

Next I'm going to fly over the ice cream factory, just to make sure we do.

Tonight we're going up to Tar Beach. Mommy is roasting peanuts and frying chicken, and Daddy will bring home a watermelon. Mr. and Mrs. Honey will bring the beer and their old green card table.

And then the stars will fall around me, and I will fly to the union building.

I'll take Be Be with me. He has threatened to tell Mommy and Daddy if I leave him behind.

I have told him it's very easy, anyone can fly. All you need
is somewhere to go that you can't get to any other way. The
next thing you know, you're flying among the stars.

Courtesy of the Solomon R. Guggenheim Museum, New York City.

Tar Beach, a story quilt by Faith Ringgold, combines autobiography, fictional narrative, painting, and quilt making in one art form. It was completed in 1988 as the first of five quilts in Ringgold's "Woman on a Bridge" series and is in the collection of the Solomon R. Guggenheim Museum in New York City.

Faith Ringgold has been a painter since the 1950s. In the 1970s she began to work in soft sculpture, collaborating with her mother, Willi Posey Jones, a fashion designer and dressmaker, who had a major influence on her interest in quilts. Willi Posey described watching her grandmother, Betsy Bingham, boil and bleach flour sacks to line the quilts she sewed. Susie Shannon, Betsy's mother, was a slave in antebellum Florida who made quilts as part of her duties. Ringgold's quilt designs echo the African-influenced, repetitive geometric design characteristic of many Early American quilts.

As Ringgold became more interested in telling stories as well as in painting and quilt making, she began using quilts as vehicles for her stories. Most of her quilts concern the experience of the Black female in America. Cassie, the narrator of *Tar Beach*, dreams of being free to go wherever she wants for the rest of her life. Flying is how she will achieve her dream, echoing an important motif in African-American folk-tale literature, in which slaves told of "flying" to freedom as wish fulfillment or as a metaphor for escaping from slavery. References to more contemporary African-American history are also part of the story. Ringgold alludes to the practice of excluding African-Americans and Native Americans from unions in her description of Cassie's father, who was not allowed in "the Union" because he was "colored or a half-breed Indian, like they say." Minorities, even those used by trades for skills such as high-steel work, could be excluded from unions on the basis of the so-called grandfather clause: if a man's father was not a union member, that was grounds for keeping him out, too. Cassie fulfills Ringgold's vision of a Black female doing heroic, creative things, for it is Cassie who has the power to emancipate her father.

But *Tar Beach* is not a work of history; it is fiction, the transformation of Ringgold's

Photo by C. Love
Courtesy of the Bernice
Steinbaum Gallery, New York City.

memories of childhood. Ringgold was born and still lives in Harlem. Her family often went up on the roof on hot summer nights. Adults played cards. Children ate and stayed up late, lying together on a mattress. The childless couples, who always seemed to have more money than the families with children, are represented by Mr. and Mrs. Honey, named because, as Ringgold says, "It was always 'honey' this and 'honey' that."

The site of *Tar Beach* is the rooftop of a neighboring apartment house that Ringgold sees from the windows of her Harlem apartment. The bridge is the George Washington Bridge, which Ringgold calls "her bridge," because it has been part of her view all of her life.

The picture book *Tar Beach* shares many elements with Ringgold's story quilt. The text, originally written on fabric strips around the border of the quilt, has been altered slightly for stylistic and textual reasons. Ringgold created entirely new paintings for the book, using acrylic on canvas paper, similar to the canvas fabric she used in the original quilt painting. The page border is reproduced from the original story quilt, and the background material for the text is the same canvas paper Ringgold used in her paintings.